Cotton Candy

The Pink Alpaca

By Uncle Dave

ISBN-13:

978-1530146857

Cotton Candy the Pink Alpaca was authored by Uncle Dave Howard, and was illustrated by Uncle Dave Howard.

Published by Uncle Dave's Books © 2016

www.uncledavesbooks.com

UncleDavesBooks.cor

Thank you Lena and Phil!
This one is for
Jenny the Cat
And the
Lippencott Alpacas!

Today was born a fuzzy little thing. "A pink alpaca" everyone did sing. It was born in the hay, on this beautiful day. Her fiber was so pink, no one ever did think that an alpaca could be that way, but it was born on this day.

(Alpaca wool is called
Fiber and fleece. It is the
alpaca's fur. Softer than
wool and less itchy too.)

All the other alpacas did stare. They looked at the pink cria there.

What could this mean? Was there something wrong?

A pink alpaca just didn't belong.

(Cria "kree-ahh" is the name for a baby Alpaca.)

The other alpacas knew, that no matter how much it grew, that they would never play, or talk to the pink cria born today.

Phil and Lena could only stare, at the pink alpaca standing there.

"Let's name her Cotton Candy," Phil said.

Lena thought. "Maybe it was something her mom was fed."

(Alpacas come in many colors; 22 colors in fact. Shades of white to brown and black. White is the most com-mon, but definitely not pink.)

They sheared off all the pink. Lena did think,

that the fiber would make a nice hat, socks, scarf or something like that.

(Alpacas are sheared for their fiber. Just like sheep's wool, it can then be combed out then spun into yarn. From that you can make lots of

things.)

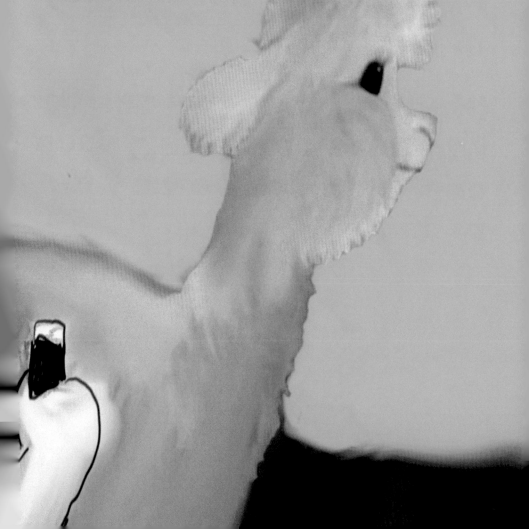

Lena took the fiber from the barn, and she made it into beautiful pink yarn.

She knitted all night and all day. She knitted and watched the alpacas play.

(Knitting uses two needles where as crocheting uses one. Both can be very fun to learn.)

All except the little pink one! She noticed it wasn't having any fun.

None of the others would play with her because of her pink fiber fur.

(Alpacas are herd animals. They like to hang out with other alpacas. If they spot danger they will make high pitch squealing noises to alert their friends.)

Lena made a beautiful pink hat, a scarf, socks and a toy for her cat.

She wore them out that day, to watch the alpacas play.

(Cats love alpaca yarn.
This is Jenny.)

A van pulled up, and men got out. They all looked and they did shout.

"An alpaca that is pink!"

They didn't know what to think.

(Alpacas are part of the Camelid family. Camelids include; Camels, llamas, Guanacos, Vicunas, and Alpacas.)

"Grab the cameras! This is going live! We are here from Channel Five!"

(Alpacas and llamas look a lot alike. Llamas have big long banana shaped ears. Llamas also are bigger with longer noses.)

The story was on all the news that day,

"This is Cotton Candy," They did say.

They showed Lena's pink hat, her socks, scarf and the toy for her cat!

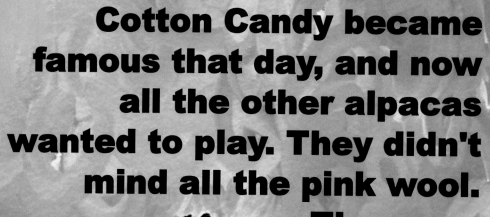

Cotton Candy became famous that day, and now all the other alpacas wanted to play. They didn't mind all the pink wool. They now think pink is cool!

Made in the USA
Lexington, KY
12 September 2018